Henry, the little hedgehog, lives in Squirrel Forest.
He has everything he could wish for, especially loving parents.
However, Henry is always complaining!

He thinks his mommy showers him with too many kisses,
his daddy never has time to play, and his little sister is just so noisy!

This morning, Henry is furious. His father refuses to take him
hunting for slugs because he is too young.

Henry scuffs his foot on the floor and sulks.
"If that's how it is, I'm leaving!" he declares. And, while his parents aren't looking, Henry sneaks out. He wants to find the perfect family.

On his way, Henry comes across Lester playing in the hay.
The little donkey's cheerfulness makes Henry feel better.
"Hi," mutters Henry. "Are you alone? Where are your parents?"

"If you like," Lester replies. "I'll take you to meet them.
But only if you stop sulking!"

Lester shows Henry two beautiful horses galloping in a meadow.
"These are my parents," says the little donkey.
"Your parents?" exclaims Henry in surprise. "But, you're not a foal!"

"Of course not," replies Lester. "I was adopted.
And believe me, I couldn't be happier!"
Henry nods. And then he continues on his way.

A little later, he spots a frog singing a delightful song. The little frog is singing a nursery rhyme and Henry likes the tune. "Hello," he says.

"Did your family teach you to sing? You're very talented!"
"Thank you," replies the frog. "My name's Fiona. If you come with me, I'll teach you the song."

The little frog leads Henry to a big water lily.
"This is my mother and this is where we live," explains Fiona.

"Do you have a daddy?" asks Henry. "Who protects you at night?"
"Mommy does, of course!" Fiona tells him. "And believe me,
with mommy around the toads had better behave themselves!"

After a good laugh, Henry continues on his way.

He approaches a farm where some pigs are rolling around
in the mud. One of the pigs, Percy, doesn't look like the others.
"Hello," says Henry. "Why aren't you pink like your friends?"

"Oh, that's an easy question!" replies Percy.
"My daddy isn't a pig! He's a wild boar!"

"I come from the farm and my husband comes from the forest," explains Percy's mommy. "And ever since he was born, our son has been used to our different ways of life!"

"Exactly!" exclaims Percy. "I eat both acorns and corn! I'm half-boar and half-pig."

Henry is amazed. These families are so different!
The little hedgehog realizes that he has a lot to learn from life.

It's time for Henry to move on. Soon he feels his tummy rumbling. Henry is hungry. He would happily eat some lettuce or an earthworm!

"Hello there," says someone. "Are you lost?"
It's Calvin, a young calf, who kindly invites
Henry home for lunch.

"This is my daddy, Roger. He is the strongest of all the bulls,"
Calvin proudly tells him. "And this is Barnaby, my other daddy!"

"Do you mean that you have two daddies?" Henry asks.
"I didn't know that was possible!"
"Of course it is!" Calvin explains. "I'm not much different from you because I have two parents too!"

After a delicious meal, Henry continues on his way.
He is not far from a village when he meets Celia,
a little swallow.
The hedgehog is surprised to see that Celia shares
a nest with an old owl.
"Mama Betsy," says Celia. "Can I play outside with
the hedgehog?"
"Of course you can," Mama Betsy replies.

Henry sits down on the grass next to his new friend.
"You know," Celia explains. "Betsy isn't really my mama.
She's my nanny. She looks after me when mommy and daddy
are working."

After listening to Celia, Henry realizes that he really misses his mommy's kisses. And even if his daddy doesn't take him hunting for slugs at least he gets to see him every day!

"I'm beginning to wonder if the perfect family really exists?" says Henry.
"I know a perfect family!" shouts Victor, the little wolf hiding in the bushes. "It's mine!"

"Wolves live in packs," explains Victor. "So, I've not only got a daddy and a mommy, I also have three step-fathers, seven step-mothers, and about thirty brothers and sisters! Imagine the commotion when it's time for bed!"

Henry isn't really convinced that Victor's family is
his idea of perfect. One little sister is enough for him!
He even misses her, too.

Henry decides to head home. Luckily, the return journey isn't very long. He is so excited to see his family. Henry, the little hedgehog, realizes what he has learned during his travels — the perfect family doesn't exist.

He also learned that nothing is more important
or special than... **LOVE!**

General Director: Gauthier Auzou
Senior Editor: Claire Simon
English Version Editor: Rebecca Frazer
Layout: Annaïs Tassone
Translation from French: Susan Allen Maurin
Original title: *Camille veut une nouvelle famille*
© Auzou Publishing, Paris (France), 2014 (English version)
ISBN: 978-2-7338-2704-8

Printed and bound in China, December 2013.